MARTINS FERRY P.L. (MFP
3 3667 00304 8680
W9-AQA-841

LIBRARIAN REVIEWER
Laurie K. Holland
Media Specialist (National Board Certified), Edina, MN
MA in Elementary Education, Minnesota State University, Mankato, MN

READING CONSULTANT
Elizabeth Stedem
Educator/Consultant, Colorado Springs, CO
MA in Elementary Education, University of Denver, CO

Graphic Sparks are published by Stone Arch Books,
151 Good Counsel Drive, P.O. Box 669,
Mankato, Minnesota 56002.
*www.stonearchbooks.com*



*Library of Congress Cataloging-in-Publication Data*
Temple, Bob.
Jimmy Sniffles: A Nose for Danger / by Bob Temple; illustrated by Steve Harpster.
p. cm. — (Graphic Sparks)
ISBN-13: 978-1-59889-036-5 (hardcover)
ISBN-10: 1-59889-036-0 (hardcover)
1. Graphic novels. I. Harpster, Steve. II. Title. III. Series.
PN6727.T2945J56 2006
741.5—dc22 2005026686

Summary: Jimmy Sniffles is allergic — to danger! ACHOOOO! A bag of diamonds is missing from the local jewelry store, and Jimmy, with his super-snotty schnozz, saves the day.

Art Director: Heather Kindseth
Production Manager: Sharon Reid
Production/Design: James Liebman, Mie Tsuchida
Production Assistance: Bob Horvath, Eric Murray

1 2 3 4 5 6 11 10 09 08 07 06

Printed in the United States of America.

# JIMMY SNIFFLES
# A NOSE FOR DANGER

BY BOB TEMPLE

ILLUSTRATED BY STEVE HARPSTER

STONE ARCH BOOKS
Minneapolis San Diego

CAST OF CHARACTERS
ROBBER 1
ROBBER 2
NEWS ANCHOR
55
MRS. WINKLE

JIMMY'S DAD
JIMMY'S MOM
JIMMY'S NOSE
JIMMY SNIFFLES

Meet Jimmy Sniffles . . .

Meet Jimmy's nose . . .

Jimmy might think that his life is boring . . .

. . . but his nose knows better!

One day Jimmy Sniffles is shopping with his mom.
Mom, can we go now?
Be patient, Jimmy. I'm almost done.
Don't you just love this style? I'll wear these shoes on Wednesdays!
Um, yeah. Great. Can we go now?
How come nothing exciting ever happens to me?
BIG SHOE SALE

Just three more stops, and we'll be all done with my errands!
Three more stops?
EARL'S JEWELRY
Stop! Thieves! They've got our precious gems! Somebody call 9-1-1!
Just then, Jimmy's nose smells danger.
AAACHOOO!

CHOOOOOOOOO
My, what a sneeze! You must have an allergy.
4GH-8
HONK

Run!
Let's get out of here!
Did you hear something?
Only you sneezing, dear.
BAM
ACHOOOO!

Ooof!
I think you sneezed so hard . . .
. . . you made the car move!
Not funny, Mom.
MACK

Leave it. We'll get it later.

Mom! Look what I found!
That's nice, dear.
Oh please, let it be something exciting.
Oh please! Oh please!

Oh please, let it be . . .
. . . rocks.
A bunch of dumb rocks.
Rocks? Who would put a bunch of dumb rocks in a nice bag like this?
14

Aw . . .
Rocks!

Some kids find money on the ground.
Some kids find cool agates or marbles.
Some kids find baby bunnies or kittens or something.

I find a bag
of dumb rocks.

Why can't
one exciting thing
ever happen
to me?

Jimmy,
I've got a fun
idea! Let's sort
the laundry!

If we work together, it should only take an hour or so . . .
Nooooooooo!!!

In a daring daytime robbery, two masked burglars stole several bags containing priceless gems. . . .
Remember to fold your underpants, Jimmy. Don't just throw them into a pile!
. . . It is believed that the robbers dropped one of the bags during their escape. . . .
Looks like we need to get you some new socks.
Ooooh. Really exciting, Dad.

. . . The bag is a small, brown velvet bag, tied with a yellow ribbon. It contains five or six gems. . . .
AH AAAH AAAH AAAH AAAH
. . . These gems are unpolished, so they look like ordinary rocks. If you have found this bag, call the police immediately. . . .
. . . The robbers are armed and ***dangerous***, and they will likely try to recover the lost bag.
AAAHH
CHOO

That night, Jimmy has to go to his brother's band concert at the middle school. But he is not alone.
You sure that's the kid?
Yeah. I can see the bag in his pocket.
I think I can reach between the seats.
Uh-oh. I smell something funny.

Now just hold still, little fella . . .
AACHOOOOO
Sorry!

The next day . . .
Okay, let's hear "Mary Had a Little Lamb" one more time.
Again?
Are you ready? Play.
Cel-lo is so darn bor-ing, darn bor-ing, darn bor-ing.
Cel-lo is so darn bor-ing, it makes me want to barf.
I think I might be able to reach . . .
Just a . . . little . . . farther . . .

AAAAAA!
CHOOOOOOOOOOOOO
Mrs. Winkle, I don't think I can continue my cello lesson!

Robbers still at large . . .
Lots of excitement.
. . . Police believe the crooks will try to recover the missing bag of gems. . .
Band concert. Cello lessons.
. . . Anyone who has found a brown velvet bag with a yellow ribbon should call the police immediately. . . .
And sneezing. Lots of sneezing!

. . . These robbers are armed and ***dangerous***.
My life is soooo boring!
Jimmy! It's time to go to your sister's dance recital!
See what I mean.

Why don't we just jump him and take the bag?
In front of all these people? Not a chance.
BACKSTAG
Mom, how long before this is over?
The Grand Finale is next!

Grand Finale! Everybody on stage!
What should we do?
Dance, I guess.
I don't remember any dances with thieves in them. Do you, Jimmy?
ACHOOO
ACHOOO
ACHOOO

The next day, Jimmy goes to his brother's soccer game.
Everything is so boring. I wish these rocks were interesting.
But I guess not. Just a stupid bag of rocks.

BAM

ACHOOOO!

In a daring capture, young Jimmy Sniffles threw himself at the robbers, knocking them out cold.
Police
55
Both thieves were taken into custody.
And young Jimmy Sniffles is being heralded as a hero. Back to you, Susan.
55
55

NEWS
5
Hey kid,
nice work.
Huh?
NEWS
5
Police
Hey, I think
my allergy
cleared up.
Until next time!
END

Bob Temple has never found a bag of stolen gems, and he's never solved a crime by sneezing, but he has written more than 30 books for children.

Steve Harpster has loved to draw funny cartoons, mean monsters, and goofy gadgets since he was able to pick up a pencil. In first grade, he was able to avoid his writing assignments by working on the pictures for the stories instead.

Steve landed a job drawing funny pictures for books, and that's really what he's best at. Steve lives in Columbus, Ohio, with his wonderful wife, Karen, and their sheepdog, Doodle.

**agate** (AG-it) a stone with bands of color inside

**allergy** (AL-ur-jee) a bad reaction, such as sneezing, to things like dust, pollen, food, or homework

**boring** (BOR-ing) doing laundry, watching your brother's band concert or your sister's dance recital, and just about anything else that you ***have*** to do

**errand** (AIR-uhnd) going to a place to do something, such as buying a pair of shoes; adults always have errands to do, especially on weekends when they could take you to the zoo or a water park.

**gem** (JEM) a valuable stone, such as a diamond or ruby

**underpants** (UHN-dur-pantss) the adult word for underwear; it's easy to remember, kids wear underwear, and adults wear underpants.

Oooh! They look so nice and shiny! Maybe I could polish up my vocabulary with some of these words!

# Silly Sneezing Snippets

Can't understand what your doctor is talking about? That's because doctors know the fancy scientific names for everything. When you're sneezing, your doctor says you're ***sternutating*** (STUR-nyoo-tay-ting). And a ***sternutator*** (STUR-nyoo-tay-tur) is something that causes you to sneeze.

When you sneeze, your eyes close. If they didn't, or if you held your eyes open, they could pop out. Honest.

The air from a sneeze rushes out your nose at 100 miles per hour!

Bright lights can make some people sneeze.

If you sneeze too hard, you can break a rib. Ouch!

Donna Griffiths of the United Kingdom began sneezing in 1981. She didn't stop until 978 days later. She holds the Guinness World Record for longest sneezing attack. She must have needed a lot of tissues!

1.) Jimmy doesn't see all the exciting things that happen around him. Why?

2.) Jimmy didn't listen to the news on TV. If he had, he would have realized that the boring rocks he found were really diamonds. If Jimmy had found out, what do you think he would have done with the jewels?

3.) At the beginning of the story, Jimmy doesn't like being allergic to things. Do you think, after he learns about the robbers and jewels, that he will be glad he's allergic?

1.) Jimmy hates shopping with his mom. Write about an activity that your mom and dad make you do that is boring. Is there something you could do to make it exciting?

2.) At the end of the story, Jimmy is a hero, except he doesn't know why. Pretend you are Jimmy's friend who has seen everything. Write down what he missed.

3.) While you're out shopping with your family, some careless robbers drop something valuable next to you. Write what you would do next.

Do you want to know more about subjects related to this book? Or are you interested in learning about other topics? Then check out FactHound, a fun, easy way to find Internet sites.

Our investigative staff has already sniffed out great sites for you!

Here's how to use FactHound:

1.) Visit *www.facthound.com*

2.) Select your grade level.

3.) To learn more about subjects related to this book, type in the book's ISBN number: ***1598890360***. If you're looking for information on another subject, simply type in a keyword.

4.) Click the ***Fetch It*** button.

FactHound will fetch the best Internet sites for you.